Rosie Rudey

and the Enormous Chocolate Mountain

Sarah Naish and Rosie Jefferies

Illustrated by Megan Evans

Jessica Kingsley Publishers
London and Philadelphia

First published in 2018
by Jessica Kingsley Publishers
73 Collier Street
London N1 9BE, UK
and
400 Market Street, Suite 400
Philadelphia, PA 19106, USA

www.jkp.com

Library of Congress Cataloging in Publication Data
A CIP catalog record for this book is available from the Library of Congress

British Library Cataloguing in Publication Data
A CIP catalogue record for this book is available from the British Library

ISBN 978 1 78592 302 9
eISBN 978 1 78450 612 4

Printed and bound in China

Introduction
Meet Rosie Rudey and her family

Rosie Rudey lives with her mum, dad, brother William Wobbly, and sisters, Sophie Spikey, Katie Careful and Charley Chatty. The children did not have an easy start in life and now live with their new mum and dad. All the stories are true stories. The children are real children who had difficult times, and were left feeling as if they could not trust grown-ups to sort anything out, or look after them properly. Sometimes the children were sad, sometimes very angry. Often they did things which upset other people but they did not understand why.

In this story, Rosie has a fuzzy feeling in her tummy. She has spotted a lot of chocolate in the kitchen and knows this will help her to stop feeling fuzzy. Rosie makes a beautiful chocolate mountain in her bedroom and feels she must eat quite a lot. Now she is feeling a bit ill though, and it's dinner time! What will she do? Luckily, Rosie's new mum is good at spotting when Rosie is feeling fuzzy and is able to help her sort it out.

Written by Rosie's mum, and Rosie (who is a grown up now), this story will help everyone feel a bit better.

Sometimes Rosie Rudey was very rude to her new mum and dad. She didn't like people helping her and always used her grumpy, squished up face to keep people away. Her brother and sisters, Katie, William, Sophie and Charley, annoyed Rosie quite a lot. She liked being VERY bossy to them.

When Katie annoyed Rosie, she felt a fuzzy feeling in her tummy.

When Sophie teased her about her grumpy, meany face, she felt the fuzzy feeling too.

When Charley Chatty got Mum's attention, her tummy felt VERY fuzzy.

When Rosie felt fuzzy, she was very grumpy...even more grumpy than normal!

Rosie wondered which was bigger in her tummy: grumpiness or fuzziness.

William said she was the greediest. Sometimes Rosie did not like William very much.

When it was lovely food time, Rosie forgot about being rude and stamping about quite so much. Rosie thought about eating lovely things ALL THE TIME!

Rosie's very best 'lovely food' was chocolate. She quite liked cakes and biscuits, but Rosie would do ANYTHING to get chocolate. She would even be polite and smiley to her mum. Chocolate made her feel all warm and cosy, her tummy smiled and the fuzziness went away.

Today, Mum was busy sorting out William and Katie who were arguing about who had the biggest space on the sofa. Rosie noticed that everyone's chocolate Easter eggs had been left out on the kitchen table. Mum always let them have a bit each day but Rosie wanted ALL of hers. Right now!

Rosie concentrated very hard on walking slowly so nobody noticed what she was doing. As she walked past the Easter eggs, her hand suddenly picked two up.

Rosie held the eggs stiffly at her side and slid past the others so they did not see what she was doing.

When she had walked past them she rushed as fast as she could to her bedroom, and hid the chocolate under her bed.

All that rushing about had made Rosie very hungry again, so she quickly ate one WHOLE chocolate egg as fast as she could.

Rosie realised that everyone was still busy being cross, so she suddenly found her legs rushing back to the kitchen to take the rest of the Easter eggs!

Rosie only just had time to hide the other three eggs when she heard Mum say it was 'pocket money time'. Rosie was pleased as she knew she could buy another bar of chocolate in the little shop.

While Mum got everyone ready to go shopping, Rosie checked that the other chocolate eggs were still safe. She could feel her tummy calling out for emergency chocolate, so she quickly stuffed another bit in and made sure she had swallowed it all before she came out of her room.

At the shop they all bought one bar of chocolate each, apart from Sophie. As usual, she bought a bag of tiny sweets. Rosie knew this was so Sophie could eat them very slowly and show off that she still had some left later on.

Mum told everyone she would keep the chocolate until after dinner as that was 'the rule'. Rosie did not like the rules. She said rudely, "Why do you always get to keep the stupid chocolate? I am hungry NOW!"

Mum smiled at Rosie and said she could have an apple for now if she was hungry.

Rosie thought Mum was very annoying.

When they got home, Rosie noticed that Mum had put all of the chocolates in the tin. When Mum went to the toilet, Rosie quickly found she had accidentally taken all of the bars of chocolate.

Rosie rushed upstairs before anyone saw her. She added the chocolate bars to the pile of Easter eggs. It was too big to fit under her bed now, so Rosie pulled it all out and made a lovely pile of chocolate in the middle of her bedroom.

Rosie looked at her pile and thought it looked beautiful. In fact, she thought it looked like an enormous chocolate mountain! Rosie felt a warm, happy feeling in her tummy and sat down next to the chocolate mountain. It all looked so lovely, and Rosie's tummy felt so fuzzy that she started eating the chocolate bars. This made Rosie feel very happy so she thought she had better eat some Easter eggs as well.

Suddenly Rosie realised that there was NO CHOCOLATE LEFT!

She heard Mum calling her for dinner, but when she stood up she felt a swooshing, sicky feeling in her tummy. "Oh no," she thought, "how am I going to fit my dinner in as well?"

Rosie rushed downstairs and pretended she needed to get her bike in from the garden.

In the garden the swooshy, sicky feeling swirled out of her tummy and onto the grass in a big pile of chocolatey sick.

Rosie realised that Mum was standing next to her. Rosie's ears went hot and she stepped away from Mum.

Mum said, "Oh dear Rosie, it looks like you are not well. That sick looks very chocolatey. I wonder if that's where the chocolate from the tin and the Easter eggs went?"

Rosie stood very still and quiet. Her head made some humming noises.

Mum continued, "Sometimes, when children have felt frightened and muddly when they were very little, they feel like they have a big, fuzzy, hungry space in their tummy ALL the time. Their brain tells them they need to eat lots of sugar and chocolate to fill it up and make the fuzzy feeling go away. But shall I tell you a secret?"

Rosie shrugged her shoulders and said "Don't care!"

(But she DID care.)

Luckily Mum knew she cared really so carried on, "Well, it doesn't matter if you eat a thousand bars of chocolate, you will still have that empty, hungry space in your tummy."

Rosie looked sadly at the chocolatey sick pile and realised she still felt hungry.

Mum put her arm around Rosie and explained, "Do you know? That big, empty space can start to feel fuller by having hugs. You can even make it smaller yourself by rushing about a bit. It's like magic!"

Rosie did not like the sound of the 'rushing about' bit but she DID like the sound of hugs filling up the fuzzy, empty space.

As they went back inside, Mum kept her arm around Rosie while she suggested ways for her to help get the chocolate that she had 'accidentally' taken from the others back.

Later that night in bed, Rosie thought about how nice Mum's arm had felt giving her a hug. She wondered if that had made the big, empty space a bit smaller yet.

She thought she still had an empty space inside though...

Just about the size of a chocolate bar.

The End

A note for parents and carers, from the authors

This book was written to help you to help your child. All the children in the stories are based on real children and life events.

Rosie Rudey has many of the behavioural and emotional issues experienced by children who have suffered developmental trauma and therefore has attachment difficulties. You will see in this book that Rosie craves sugar and is unable to sense when she has had too much. This is often because our children have high levels of cortisol and want sugar to relieve the feelings associated with that. Rosie described these feelings as 'fuzziness', which is distinct from hunger. Often, our children are unable to correctly identify feelings of hunger, especially where there has been neglect in early life.

We provide training to therapeutic parents (such as adopters and foster carers), who have told us that they often feel out of their depth, and don't know what to say or do when faced with these issues. This story not only gives you valuable insight into WHY our children behave this way, but also enables you to read helpful words, through a third party therapeutic parent, to your child to explain their feelings and resulting behaviours. This helps them to feel safe and to start to manage their own behaviours.

The illustrations in the book are deliberately simple. This allows your child to stay focused on the message within the story, without being distracted by small unimportant details. We are also careful to ensure Rosie's siblings appear in the background of the story so children do not worry where they might be.

This story not only names feelings for the child, but also gives parents and carers therapeutic parenting strategies within the story. It features some techniques which you can try in your own family:

- **Using 'parental presence' or touch to regulate** – Many of our children function at a much younger emotional age, and never learned to control their emotions (self-regulate) as young babies. When our children are very upset, frightened or spiralling out of control, simply being near them or next to them can help them to regulate. We do not need to say anything. Holding hands or placing a calm hand on the child's shoulder can also help them to calm and to self-regulate. In this story Mum touches Rosie on her shoulder and also puts her arm around her. This kind of touch is not expected to be reciprocated, but carries a powerful message of reassurance and acceptance.

- **Naming the need** - Therapeutic parents look carefully at behaviours and think about where they may have come from. We then try to relate the behaviours to the underlying cause to help the child to make sense of their own thoughts, feelings and behaviours. This is one of the most empowering things we can do as therapeutic parents. This story uses 'naming the need' to explain where Rosie's feeling of emptiness might come from and explains the compulsion to fill that emptiness with sugar. Mum also gives Rosie some strategies to help her to manage these feelings. "That big, empty space can start to feel fuller by having hugs. You can even make it smaller yourself by rushing about a bit. It's like magic!"

- **Consistency** – Therapeutic parents maintain consistency by keeping strong routines, boundaries and structure. Towards the end of the story we see Mum starting to address how Rosie can make amends for her actions, suggesting ways for Rosie to help get the chocolate back.

- **Wondering aloud** – Therapeutic parents use 'wondering aloud' to help to identify reasons, without asking the child 'why'. In this story Mum uses 'wondering aloud' to avoid asking a direct question of Rosie while she is dysregulated. "I wonder if that's where the chocolate from the tin and the Easter eggs went?"

- **Empathy and nurture** – Even when Rosie has clearly taken chocolate and made herself sick through eating so much, Mum concentrates on the underlying issues first and demonstrates empathy by expressing concern about her daughter's well-being, "It looks like you are not well."

Sarah is a therapeutic parent of five adopted siblings, now all adults, CEO of the National Association of Therapeutic Parents (NATP), former social worker and previous owner of an 'Outstanding' therapeutic fostering agency. Rosie is her daughter, and checked and amended the character's thoughts and expressed feelings to ensure they are as accurate a reflection as possible.

Together, Rosie and Sarah now spend all their time working within the NATP, and Fostering Attachments Ltd training and helping parents, carers, social workers and other professionals to heal traumatised children.

Please use this story to make connections, explain behaviours and build attachments between your child and yourself.

Therapeutic parenting makes everything possible.

Warmest regards,

Sarah Naish and Rosie Jefferies

If you liked Rosie Rudey, why not meet Callum Kindly, Charley Chatty, William Wobbly, Sophie Spikey and Katie Careful

Callum Kindly and the Very Weird Child

A story about sharing your home with a new child

Katie Careful and the Very Sad Smile

A story about anxious and clingy behaviour

Charley Chatty and the Disappearing Pennies

A story about lying and stealing

William Wobbly and the Mysterious Holey Jumper

A story about fear and coping

William Wobbly and the Very Bad Day

A story about when feelings become too big

Rosie Rudey and the Very Annoying Parent

A story about a prickly child who is scared of getting close

Charley Chatty and the Wiggly Worry Worm

A story about insecurity and attention-seeking

Sophie Spikey Has a Very Big Problem

A story about refusing help and needing to be in control